Not Quite
NARWHAL

W9-AXP-316

For Harry and Mary Ellen,
who always brought rainbows into my life

No part of this publication may be reproduced, stored in a retrieval system, or transmitted in any form or by any means, electronic, mechanical, photocopying, recording, or otherwise, without written permission of the publisher.
For information regarding permission, write to Simon & Schuster Books for Young Readers,
an imprint of Simon & Schuster Children's Publishing Division, 1230 Avenue of the Americas, New York, NY 10020.

ISBN 978-1-338-28370-9

Copyright © 2017 by Jessie Sima. All rights reserved.
Published by Scholastic Inc., 557 Broadway, New York, NY 10012,
by arrangement with Simon & Schuster Books for Young Readers,
an imprint of Simon & Schuster Children's Publishing Division.
SCHOLASTIC and associated logos are trademarks and/or registered trademarks of Scholastic Inc.

The publisher does not have any control over and does not assume any responsibility for author or third-party websites or their content.

12 11 10 9 8 7 6 5 4 3 2 1   18 19 20 21 22 23

Printed in the U.S.A.   40

First Scholastic printing, January 2018

Book design by Lizzy Bromley
The text for this book was set in ITC Lubalin Graph.
The illustrations for this book were rendered in Adobe Photoshop.

Not Quite NARWHAL

JESSIE SIMA

SCHOLASTIC INC.

Kelp was born deep in the ocean.

He knew early on that he was different from the other narwhals.

His tusk wasn't as long as everyone else's,

he had different tastes in food,

and he wasn't a very good swimmer.

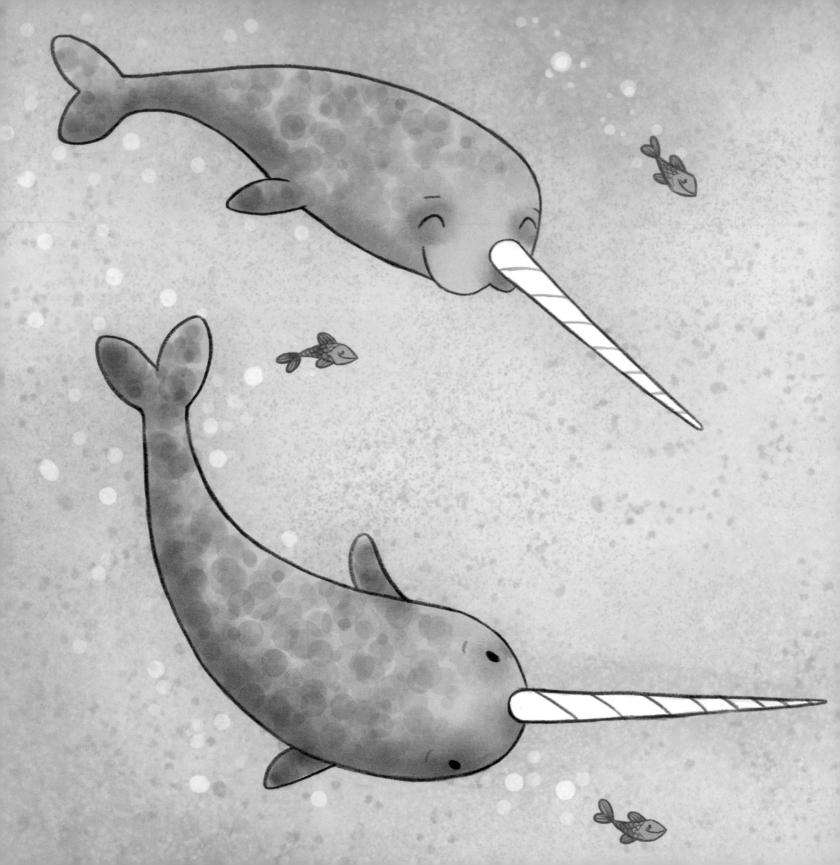

But his friends didn't seem to mind,
so Kelp decided he wouldn't either.

That is, until he was swept away by a strong current.

Kelp found himself at the surface, closer to land than he'd ever been before.

High up on a cliff he spotted a mysterious, sparkling creature.
It looked so familiar. It looked like . . . Kelp!

Kelp swam
toward land as
fast as he
could,

which wasn't
very fast
at all,

hoping that he
could catch up
with the creature
that looked just
like him.

When he finally reached the shore,
Kelp felt a little bit anxious—he had never left the ocean.

He was nervous about walking for the first time,
but the land creatures made it look so easy!

It wasn't.

Eventually he got the hang of it.

Everything on land was strange and beautiful—
but also kind of scary.

Kelp began to think
he might never find
the creature that looked
just like him. But as he
stumbled out of the forest . . .

Kelp had never heard of unicorns before. They taught him all sorts of new things about his tusk,

they introduced him to unicorn delicacies,

and they showed him how to gallop.

There was no doubt that Kelp was, in fact, a unicorn.
He was having so much fun that he didn't want to leave.

But then he remembered all of his
friends under the sea.

Kelp missed them terribly,
so he said good-bye to the unicorns
and returned to the ocean.

Kelp swam
toward home as
fast as
he could,

which wasn't
very fast at all,

hoping that the
narwhals would still
like him now that he
was a unicorn.

When he finally arrived, Kelp had butterflies in his stomach.

Kelp took a deep breath and told his friends the news.

Kelp was happy to be home, but now that he'd experienced life on land with the unicorns, he couldn't seem to forget them.

Did he want to be a land narwhal
with the unicorns . . .

or a sea unicorn with the narwhals?
Kelp couldn't decide.

But then he realized that maybe . . .

just maybe . . .

he didn't have to choose.

Jessie Sima

grew up unaware that
she was an author-illustrator.
Once she figured it out,
she told her family and friends.
They took it quite well.

Not Quite Narwhal

is her very first book.

Author photo by VICTOR SIMA